MARVIN,
THE MOSS-EATING
MOOSE

By Marte Franklin

Illustrations by Victoria Krause

Marte Franklin

Forest Friends Books

Published by E. Blok Press

MARVIN THE MOSS-EATING MOOSE

Forest Friends Books
Published by E. Blok Press

martejsb@netzero.com

M. Franklin
555 East Arrellaga Street, Suite B
Santa Barbara, CA   93103

Printed in the United States by Kindle Direct Publishing.

ISBN: 13 978-0-578-56094-6

This book is dedicated to children everywhere

Inspiration for the book

Cristi Franklin

MAMA MARVIN CURLY

MRS. WOLF MRS. GRIZZLY

& PUPS & CUBS

Marvin was born in the far North Country in early spring when there was still some snow on the ground. Other moose calves were also born around that same time, but Marvin was the smallest of all the new-born calves.

One day he told his Mama that the other calves would not let him play with them because he was so small. His Mama snuggled him and whispered, "Marvin, you will grow up to be a big fine moose, but if you do some good deeds you will grow faster."

2

Marvin looked at her and asked, "What are good deeds?

"Good deeds are ways you help others. You might see something that needs to be done, and you quietly do it without having to be told to do so. You have many forest friends. Surely you could help someone." Marvin hung his head and wandered away to rest in a patch of new green grass.

He wondered what he, a very small moose, could do to help his forest friends. Maybe he could help his Mama. He tried to think of other ways to do good deeds. He stood up and stretched and then remembered that he and Mama always slept in the same place at night. Maybe he could help her by cleaning up some of the brush around that area.

4

So off he went into the very edge of the forest
and soon he had dragged away many small
branches that had fallen into their sleeping area.
Now the area was nice and clean.   He told himself
he would not tell his Mama what he had done.

He started to go back to Mama when he heard a sound like someone crying.   He found Mrs. Wolf looking for her youngest pup.   "He was right behind the other three pups, but he is smaller and slower than the others and must have been left behind.   Can you help me find him?"

6

I am a little taller than you so perhaps I can see farther. I will help you look for him." Mrs. Wolf was so glad for the help, she said she would take the other pups back to her den and hoped Marvin would find the little guy.

Marvin searched the nearby forest. There were many places a small pup could be. He looked under some bushes and behind rocks, and soon found the pup curled up in a sunny spot, crying for his mother.

7

Soon the lost pup was home, and Mrs. Wolf was thankful for Marvin's help.   Marvin thought this helping others was not so hard, and he was glad that he had found the cute little pup.   Marvin went back to his Mama but didn't say anything about what he had done.   But he did have a big moose smile on this face.

Marvin usually stayed close to his Mama, but one day he wandered deeper into the forest.   He heard birds in the trees, and saw a small squirrel racing up a tree.   He wondered what it would be like to climb a tree.

9

When his tummy began to rumble, and he realized he was hungry.   Mama always pulled some green plants from the nearby pond for him to eat, but he wasn't ready to go home yet.   He was having too much fun exploring the forest.

Then he saw some small green plants growing on the rocks and trees nearby.   He wondered what they would taste like.   He took a small bite and found them tasty.

10

It wasn't too long before he heard his Mama calling him. He had stayed away a long time, and she was looking for him. He hurried home and told her about the squirrel and the tasty green plants he had eaten.

11

"Marvin, you probably were eating moss which only grows in shady places.   I guess you are still hungry though, since moss is such a small plant.   Maybe I should name you MARVIN, THE MOSS-EATING MOOSE even if moss is not a favorite food of moose." So that is how Marvin got his name.

12

His Mama took him down to the pond and soon she pulled up some long-stemmed green plants. He was glad his Mama gave him lots of the green plants to eat because he wanted to be big and strong someday. Then maybe the other young moose would let him play with them.

13

Mama and Marvin returned to the meadow where the other moose were grazing in the bright sunshine. Mama looked at Marvin as he watched the other moose calves playing.   She looked at Marvin and thought Marvin looked different somehow.

"Marvin, I do believe you have grown taller. Maybe the other moose will let you play with them now." Marvin shook his head. "I don't think so, Mama. They are still bigger, and they also make fun of me, calling me names. I don't like that." His Mama agreed that calling others names was not right, so together they wandered to a sunny place and took a nap.

Another day he wandered further into the forest than he usually did.   There he found some new plants with pretty flowers on them.   They grew on tall stalks and were reddish in color.   Carefully he bit the stalks of the flowers and headed home.   He gave them to his Mama, and she smiled, and gave him a big moose hug.

Marvin was learning all kinds of new things.   His
Mama taught him which plants were not good to eat.   She
showed him how to dig in the shallow pond to get the
good green plants that he liked so much.   He was glad to
be learning new things, but he was also sad.   He didn't
have any friends to play with.

17

It was so quiet in the trees, and he liked to just be quiet and listen to the sounds around him. He looked around when he saw something move a short distance away. It was a red fox. He thought the fox must be new to this part of the forest. He was just sitting on the ground, looking unhappy. Marvin walked quietly over to the fox, not wanting to scare him.

"Little red fox, don't be afraid of me.   You look so sad. Is there something wrong? Are you lost?"

"I'm new in this area, and I'm lonely.   My mother and I were chased away from the hills, and I don't know anyone here."

19

"Well, my name is Marvin, and sometimes I get lonely, too.   I'm such a small moose and the other young moose won't let me play with them."

"My name is Curly because my fur is different. It curls up.   Most foxes have straight fur."

"Well, now we can be friends and explore the forest together.   Let's go tell your mother you now have a new friend."

So off they went.   Curly told his mother that they were going to explore the nearby woods.   And what a good time they had learning about each other.

One day they climbed a nearby hill to enjoy the view, and it wasn't too long when they heard what sounded like someone scolding little ones.   It was Mrs. Grizzly trying to round up her three young bear cubs who wouldn't listen to her.   Finally, she sat down and hung her head.

22

Marvin asked if he and Curly could help her, and Mrs. Grizzly shook her head. "They just don't listen to me. I want to get them back in the den before it gets dark."

Curly had a great idea. Mrs. Grizzly could take one cub and he and Marvin would each round up another cub and follow her to the den.

As they hurried to the den, they saw the other young moose watching them. One of them remarked, "Isn't that Marvin? He seems to be taking charge of a grizzly cub. We usually stay away from grizzly mothers with babies. I wouldn't have thought Marvin was that brave. And he even looks bigger."

Marvin heard him and smiled to himself. Yes, he was getting bigger and stronger.

24

When the cubs were safely in the den,
Mrs. Grizzly thanked them and told them to come by
and play with the little cubs.   "You know it is a bit
unusual for bears to have three cubs, and it takes a lot
of patience to round up three active little ones."

As they left Curly asked,   "Why were you smiling so much at the other moose?"

"Well, those other moose were born about the same time I was, but I was much smaller.   They wouldn't let me play with them, and they called me names.   But Mama said that if I did good deeds, I would grow bigger and stronger.   And I am more confident with myself now. I know I am going to be big and strong."

Curly thought a while and then replied, "I'm going to do good deeds too, so I can grow up to protect my Mama." With that, Marvin and Curly almost raced down the hill laughing all the way. They knew they could do almost anything they set their minds to do, and they would help whenever they saw a need.

And so it was that a small moose and a little red fox walked into the woods knowing they could accomplish anything if they tried hard enough.
And they were pleased to know that helping others means you are also helping yourself to be stronger and wiser.

Made in the USA
Lexington, KY
11 December 2019